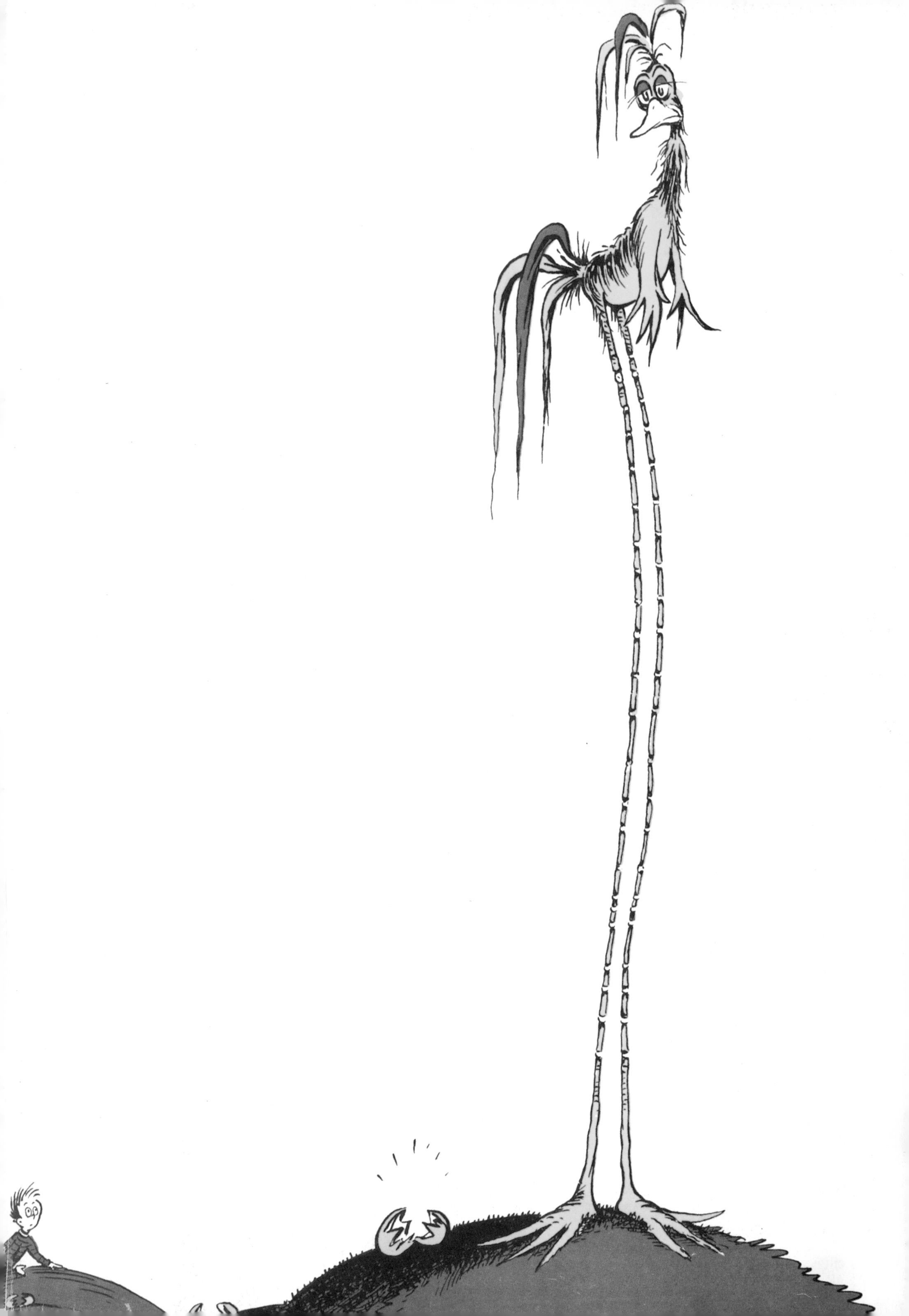

Dr. Seuss

 This collection first published in the USA by Random House, Inc., as *Dr. Seuss Storytime*. First published in the UK in 1979 by William Collins Sons & Co. This edition published in 1997 by HarperCollins*Children's Books,* a division of HarperCollins*Publishers* Ltd.

Regenerated in 1997 by Mitchell Graphics, Scotland

ISBN 0 00 195316 8

Printed and bound in Belgium

All through with the searching! All through with the looking!
I had all I needed! And now for the cooking.
I rushed to the kitchen, the place where I'd stacked 'em.
I rolled up my sleeves. I unpacked 'em and cracked 'em
And shucked 'em and chucked 'em in ninety-nine pans.
Then I mixed in some beans. I used fifty-five cans.
Then I mixed in some ginger, nine prunes and three figs
And parsley. Quite sparsely. Just twenty-two sprigs.
Then I added six cinnamon sticks and a clove.
And my scramble was ready to go on the stove!

And you know how they tasted?
They tasted just like . . .
Well, they tasted exactly
Exactly just like . . . like Scrambled eggs Super-
Dee-Dooper-dee-Booper, Special de luxe
à-la-Peter T. Hooper.

Storybook

Contents

COLLINS

McELLIGOT'S
POOL

"Young man," laughed the farmer,
"You're sort of a fool!
You'll *never* catch fish
In McElligot's Pool!"

"The pool is too small.
And, you might as well know it,
When people have junk
Here's the place that they throw it.

"You might catch a boot
Or you might catch a can.
You might catch a bottle,
But listen young man . . .
If you sat fifty years
With your worms and your wishes,
You'd grow a long beard
Long before you'd catch fishes!"

"Hmmm . . ." answered Marco,
"It *may* be you're right.
I've been here three hours
Without one single bite.
There *might* be no fish . . .

". . . But, again,
Well, there *might!*"

"'Cause you never can tell
What goes on down below!

"This pool *might* be bigger
Than you or I know!"

This MIGHT be a pool, like I've read of in books,
Connected to one of those underground brooks!

An underground river that starts here and flows
Right under the pasture! And then . . . well, *who knows?*

It *might* go along, down where no one can see,
Right under State Highway Two-Hundred-and-Three!
Right under the wagons! Right under the toes
Of Mrs. Umbroso who's hanging out clothes!

It *might* keep on flowing . . . perhaps . . . who can tell? . . .
Right under the people in Sneeden's Hotel!
Right under the grass where they're playing croquet!
Then under the mountains and far, far away!

This *might* be a river,
Now mightn't it be,

Connecting
McElligot's
Pool
With
The
Sea!

Then maybe some fish might be swimming toward me!

(If such a thing *could* be,
They certainly *would* be!)

McElligot's PooL

Some very smart fellow might point out the way
To the place where I'm fishing. And that's why I say
If I wait long enough; if I'm patient and cool,
Who knows *what* I'll catch in McElligot's Pool!

I might catch a thin fish,

I might catch a stout fish.

I might catch a short

or
a
long,
long
drawn-out fish!

Any kind! Any shape! Any colour or size!
I *might* catch some fish that would open your eyes!

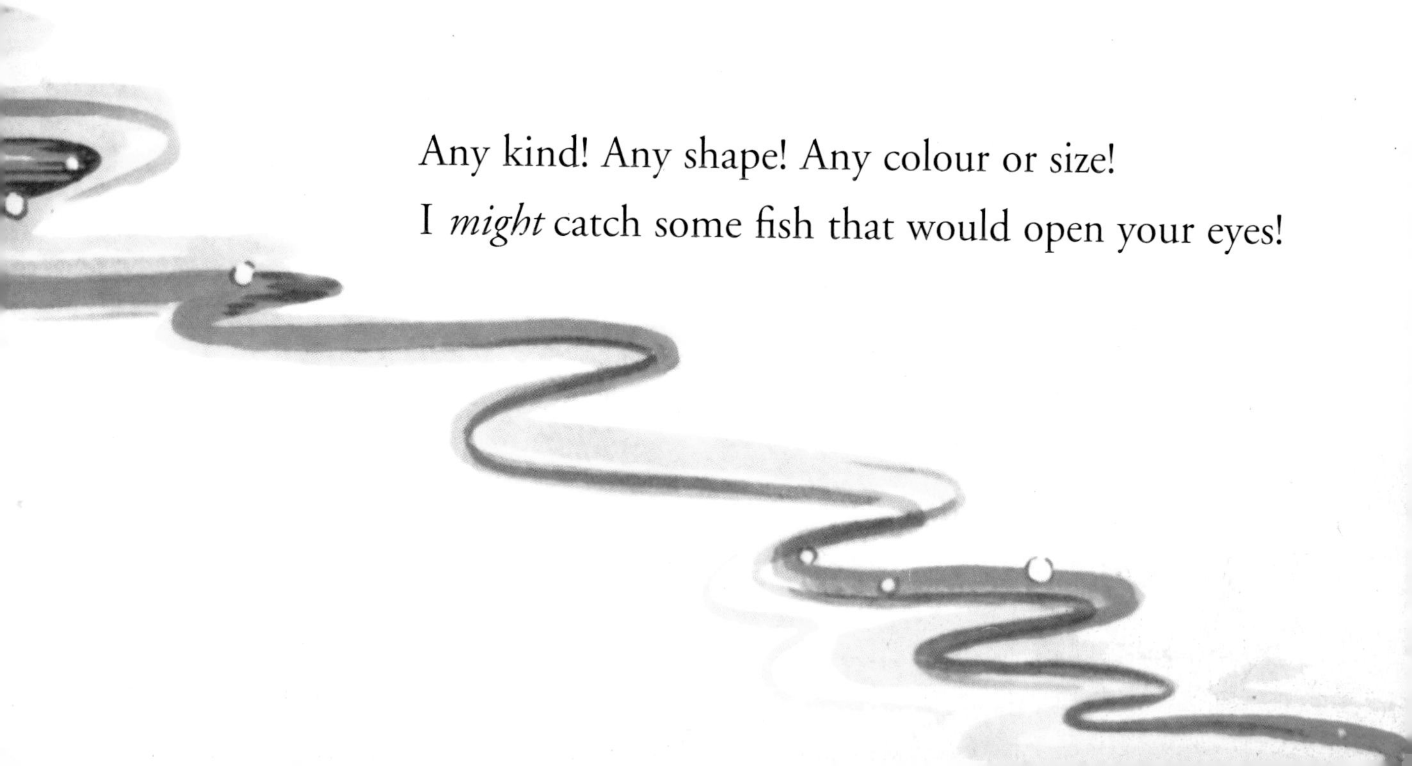

I won't be surprised if a *Dog Fish* appears!
Complete with a collar and long floppy ears!
Whoofing along! And perhaps he might chase
A whole lot of *Catfish* right straight to this place!

I might catch a fish
With a pinwheel-like tail!

I might catch a fish
Who has fins like a sail!

I might catch some young fish
Some high-jumping friskers.

I might catch an old one
With long flowing whiskers!

I might catch a fish
With a long curly nose.

I might catch a fish
Like a rooster that crows.

I might catch a fish
With a chequerboard belly,

Or even a fish
Made of strawberry jelly!

I might catch a Sea Horse.
(Now mightn't I now . . .?)

I might catch a fish
Who is partly a cow!

Some fish from the Tropics, all sunburned and hot,
Might decide to swim up!
Well they might. . .
Might they not?
Racing up north for a chance to get cool,
Full steam ahead for McElligot's Pool!

Some Eskimo Fish
From beyond Hudson Bay
Might decide to swim down;
Might be headed this way!

It's a pretty long trip,
But they *might*
And they *may.*

McELLIGOT'S POOL
4227 MILES

I might catch an eel . . .
(Well, I might. It depends.)
. . . A long twisting eel
With a lot of strange bends
And, oddly enough,
With a head on both ends!

One doesn't catch *this* kind of fish as a rule,
But the chances are fine in McElligot's Pool!

I might catch a fish
With a terrible grouch . . .

Or an Australian fish

With a kangaroo's pouch!

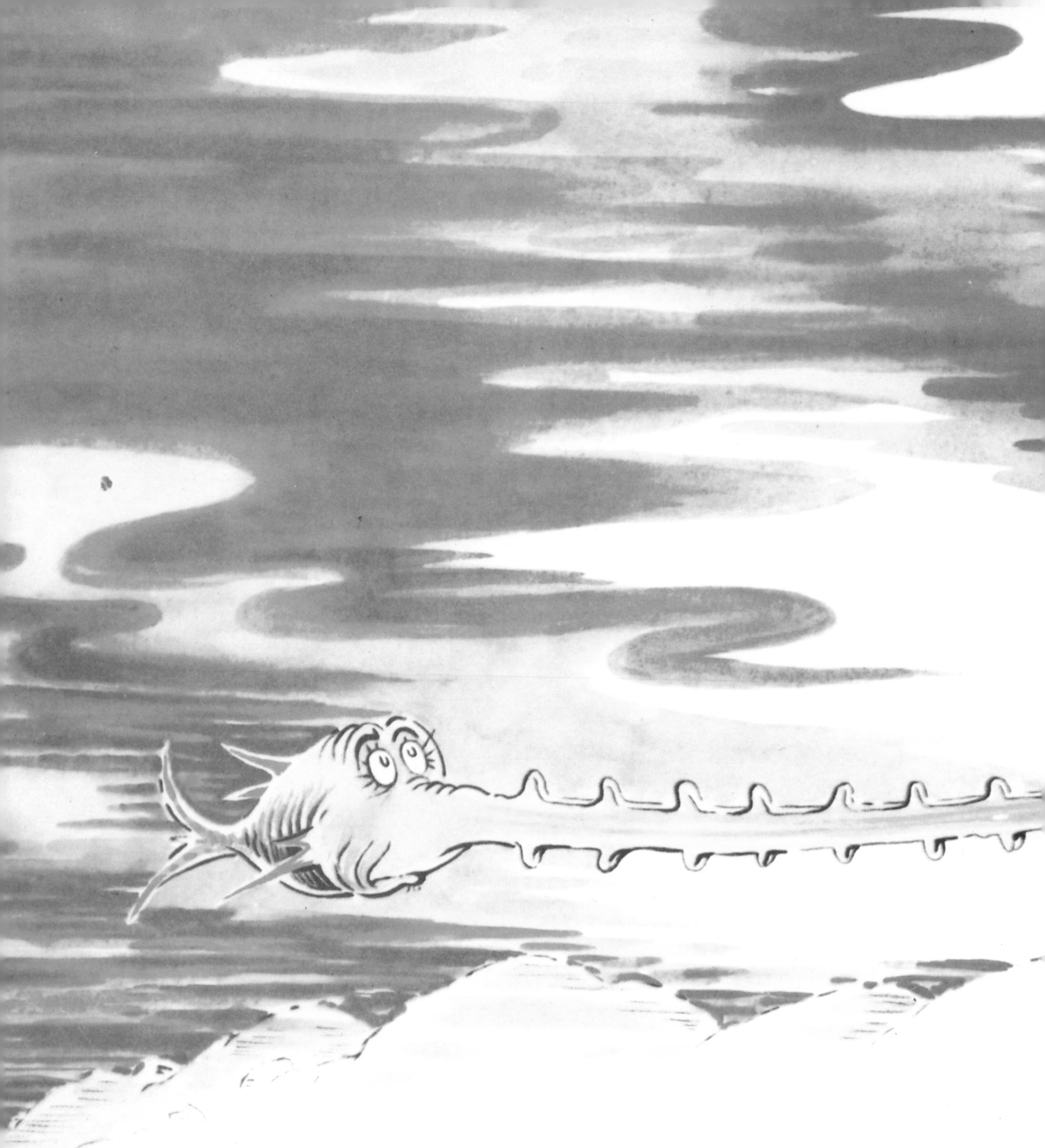

Who wants to catch small ones like mackerel or trout!
SAY! I'll catch a Saw Fish with such a long snout
That he needs an assistant to help him about!

If I wait long enough, if I'm patient and cool,
Who knows *what* I'll catch in McElligot's Pool!

Some rough-neck old Lobster,
All gristle and muscle,
Might grab at my bait,
Then would I have a tussle!

To land one so tough might take two or three hours,
But the *next* might be easy . . .

. . . The kind that likes flowers.

I *might* catch some sort of a fast-moving bloke
Who zips through the waves with an over-arm stroke!

(I *might* and I *may* and that's really no joke!)

A fish even faster!
A fish, if you please,
Who slides down the sides
Of strange islands on skis!

He *might* ski on over and pay me a visit.
That's not impossible . . . really, now is it?

Some Circus Fish!
Fish from an acrobat school,
Might stage a big show in McElligot's Pool!

Or I might catch a fish
From a stranger place yet!
From the world's highest river
In far-off Tibet,
Where the falls are so steep
That it's dangerous to ride 'em,
So the fish put on chutes
And they float down beside 'em.

From the world's deepest ocean,
From way down below,
From down in the mud where the deep-divers go,
From down in the mire and the muck and the murk,
I might catch some fish who are all going, "GLURK!"

WHALES!

I'll catch whales!

Yes, a whole herd of whales!

All spouting their spouts

And all thrashing their tails!

I'll catch fifty whales,

Then I'll stop for the day

'Cause there's *nothing* that's bigger

Than whales, so they say.

Still, of course,
It *might* be . . .

. . . that there IS something bigger!
Some sort of a kind of
A THING-A-MA-JIGGER!!

A fish that's so big, if you know what I mean,
That he makes a whale look like a tiny sardine!

Oh, the sea is so full of a number of fish,
If a fellow is patient, he *might* get his wish!

And that's why I think
That I'm not such a fool
When I sit here and fish
In McElligot's Pool!

THE ZAX

One day, making tracks
In the prairie of Prax,
Came a North-Going Zax
And a South-Going Zax.

And it happened that both of them came to a place
Where they bumped. There they stood.
Foot to foot. Face to face.
"Look here, now!" the North-Going Zax said. "I say!
You are blocking my path. You are right in my way.
I'm a North-Going Zax and I always go north.
Get out of my way, now, and let me go forth!"

"Who's in whose way?" snapped the South-Going Zax.
"I always go south, making south-going tracks.
So you're in MY way! And I ask you to move
And let me go south in my south-going groove."
Then the North-Going Zax puffed his chest up with pride.
"I never," he said, "take a step to one side.
And I'll prove to you that I won't change my ways
If I have to keep standing here fifty-nine days!"

"And I'll prove to YOU," yelled the South-Going Zax,
"That I can stand here in the prairie of Prax
For fifty-nine *years!* For I live by a rule
That I learned as a boy back in South-Going School.
Never budge! That's my rule. *Never budge in the least!*
Not an inch to the west! Not an inch to the east!
I'll stay here, not budging! I can and I will
If it makes you and me and the whole world stand still!"

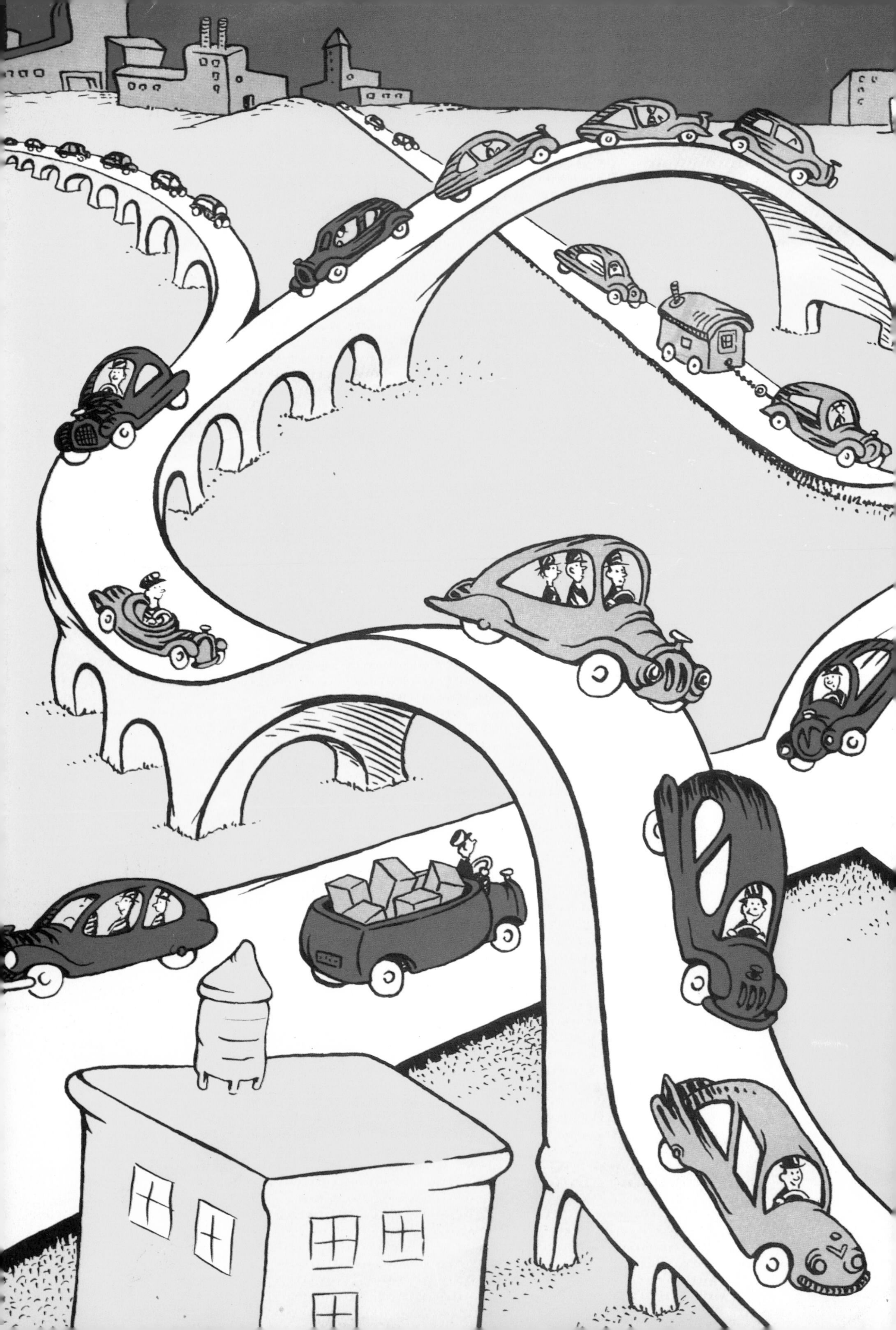

Well . . .
Of course the world *didn't* stand still. The world grew.
In a couple of years, the new highway came through
And they built it right over those two stubborn Zax
And left them there, standing un-budged in their tracks.

The LORAX

At the far end of town
where the Grickle-grass grows
and the wind smells slow-and-sour when it blows
and no birds ever sing excepting old crows . . .
is the Street of the Lifted Lorax.

And deep in the Grickle-grass, some people say,
if you look deep enough you can still see, today,
where the Lorax once stood
just as long as it could
before somebody lifted the Lorax away.

What *was* the Lorax?
And why was it there?
And why was it lifted and taken somewhere
from the far end of town where the Grickle-grass grows?
The old Once-ler still lives here.
Ask him. *He* knows.

You won't see the Once-ler.
Don't knock at his door.
He stays in his Lerkim on top of his store.
He lurks in his Lerkim, cold under the roof,
where he makes his own clothes
out of miff-muffered moof.
And on special dank midnights in August,
he peeks
out of the shutters
and sometimes he speaks
and tells how the Lorax was lifted away.

He'll tell you, perhaps...
if you're willing to pay.

The ONCE-LER

On the end of a rope
he lets down a tin pail
and you have to toss in fifteen cents
and a nail
and the shell of a great-great-great-
grandfather snail.

Then he pulls up the pail,
makes a most careful count
to see if you've paid him
the proper amount.

Then he hides what you paid him
away in his Snuvv,
his secret strange hole
in his gruvvulous glove.

Then he grunts, "I will call you by Whisper-ma-Phone,
for the secrets I tell are for your ears alone."

SLUPP!
Down slupps the Whisper-ma-Phone to your ear
and the old Once-ler's whispers are not very clear,
since they have to come down
through a snergelly hose,
and he sounds
as if he had
smallish bees up his nose.

"Now I'll tell you," he says, with his teeth sounding grey,
"how the Lorax got lifted and taken away…

It all started way back…
such a long, long time back…

Way back in the days when the grass was still green
and the pond was still wet
and the clouds were still clean,
and the song of the Swomee-Swans rang out in space . . .
one morning, I came to this glorious place.
And I first saw the trees!
The Truffula Trees!
The bright-coloured tufts of the Truffula Trees!
Mile after mile in the fresh morning breeze.

And, under the trees, I saw Brown Bar-ba-loots
frisking about in their Bar-ba-loot suits
as they played in the shade and ate Truffula Fruits.

From the rippulous pond
came the comfortable sound
of the Humming-Fish humming
while splashing around.

But those *trees!* Those *trees!*
Those Truffula Trees!
All my life I'd been searching
for trees such as these.
The touch of their tufts
was much softer than silk.
And they had the sweet smell
of fresh butterfly milk.

I felt a great leaping
of joy in my heart.
I knew what I'd do!
I unloaded my cart.

In no time at all, I had built a small shop.
Then I chopped down a Truffula Tree with one chop.
And with great skilful skill and with great speedy speed
I took the soft tuft. And I knitted a Thneed!

The instant I'd finished, I heard a *ga-Zump!*
I looked.
I saw something pop out of the stump
of the tree I'd chopped down. It was sort of a man.
Describe him? . . . That's hard. I don't know if I can.

He was shortish. And oldish.
And brownish. And mossy.
And he spoke with a voice
that was sharpish and bossy.

"Mister!" he said with a sawdusty sneeze,
"I am the Lorax. I speak for the trees.
I speak for the trees, for the trees have no tongues.
And I'm asking you, sir, at the top of my lungs"–
he was very upset as he shouted and puffed–
"What's that THING you've made out of my Truffula tuft?"

"Look, Lorax," I said. "There's no cause for alarm.
I chopped just one tree. I am doing no harm.
I'm being quite useful. This thing is a Thneed.
A Thneed's a Fine-Something-That-All-People-Need!
It's a shirt. It's a sock. It's a glove. It's a hat.
But it has *other* uses. Yes, far beyond that.
You can use it for carpets. For pillows! For sheets!
Or curtains! Or covers for bicycle seats!"

The Lorax said,
"Sir! You are crazy with greed.
There is no one on earth
who would buy that fool Thneed!"

But the very next minute I proved he was wrong.
For, just at that minute, a chap came along,
and he thought that the Thneed I had knitted was great.
He happily bought it for three ninety-eight.

I laughed at the Lorax, "You poor stupid guy!
You never can tell what some people will buy."

"I repeat," cried the Lorax,
"I speak for the trees!"

"I'm busy," I told him.
"Shut up, if you please."

I rushed 'cross the room, and in no time at all,
built a radio-phone. I put in a quick call.
I called all my brothers and uncles and aunts
and I said, "Listen here! Here's a wonderful chance
for the whole Once-ler Family to get mighty rich!
Get over here fast! Take the road to North Nitch.
Turn left at Weehawken. Sharp right at South Stitch."

And, in no time at all,
in the factory I built,
the whole Once-ler Family
was working full tilt.
We were all knitting Thneeds
just as busy as bees,
to the sound of the chopping
of Truffula Trees.

Then . . .
Oh! Baby! Oh!
How my business did grow!
Now, chopping one tree
at a time
was too slow.

So I quickly invented my Super-Axe-Hacker
which whacked off four Truffula Trees at one smacker.
We were making Thneeds
four times as fast as before!
And that Lorax? . . .
He didn't show up any more.

The
ONCE-LER-in-Chief
PRIVATE
THNEEDS
THNEEDS

But the next week
he knocked
on my new office door.

He snapped, "I'm the Lorax who speaks for the trees
which you seem to be chopping as fast as you please.
But I'm *also* in charge of the Brown Bar-ba-loots
who played in the shade of their Bar-ba-loot suits
and happily lived, eating Truffula Fruits.

"NOW . . . thanks to your hacking my trees to the ground,
there's not enough Truffula Fruit to go 'round.
And my poor Bar-ba-loots are all getting the crummies
because they have gas, and no food, in their tummies!

"They loved living here. But I can't let them stay.
They'll have to find food. And I hope that they may.
Good luck, boys," he cried. And he sent them away.

I, the Once-ler, felt sad
as I watched them all go.
BUT . . .
business is business!
And business must grow
regardless of crummies in tummies, you know.

THNEEDS
THNEEDS
YOU NEED A THNEED
NORTH
WEST
YOU NEED A THNEED
SOUTH
EAST

I meant no harm. I most truly did not.
But I had to grow bigger. So bigger I got.
I biggered my factory. I biggered my roads.
I biggered my wagons. I biggered the loads
of the Thneeds I shipped out. I was shipping them forth
to the South! To the East! To the West! To the North!
I went right on biggering . . . selling more Thneeds.
And I biggered my money, which everyone needs.

Then *again* he came back! I was fixing some pipes
when that old-nuisance Lorax came back with *more* gripes.

"I am the Lorax," he coughed and he whiffed.
He sneezed and he snuffled. He snarggled. He sniffed.
"Once-ler!" he cried with a cruffulous croak.
"Once-ler! You're making such smogulous smoke!
My poor Swomee-Swans . . . why, they can't sing a note!
No one can sing who has smog in his throat.

THNEEDS
YOU NEED A THNEED

"And so," said the Lorax,
"–please pardon my cough–
they cannot live here.
So I'm sending them off.

"Where will they go?. . .
I don't hopefully know.

They may have to fly for a month . . . or a year . . .
To escape from the smog you've smogged-up around here.

"What's *more*," snapped the Lorax. (His dander was up.)
"Let me say a few words about Gluppity-Glupp.
Your machinery chugs on, day and night without stop
making Gluppity-Glupp. Also Schloppity-Schlopp.
And what do you do with this leftover goo?. . .
I'll show you. You dirty old Once-ler man, you!

"You're glumping the pond where the Humming-Fish hummed!
No more can they hum, for their gills are all gummed.
So I'm sending them off. Oh, their future is dreary.
They'll walk on their fins and get woefully weary
in search of some water that isn't so smeary.
I hear things are just as bad up in Lake Erie."

THNEEDS

And then I got mad.
I got terribly mad.
I yelled at the Lorax, "Now listen here, Dad!
All you do is yap-yap and say, 'Bad! Bad! Bad! Bad!
Well, I have my rights, sir, and I'm telling *you*
I intend to go on doing just what I do!
And, for your information, you Lorax, I'm figgering
on biggering

and BIGGERING

and BIGGERING

and BIGGERING,

turning MORE Truffula Trees into Thneeds
which everyone, EVERYONE, *EVERYONE* needs!"

And at that very moment, we heard a loud whack!
From outside in the fields came a sickening smack
of an axe on a tree. Then we heard the tree fall.
The very last Truffula Tree of them all!

No more trees. No more Thneeds. No more work to be done.
So, in no time, my uncles and aunts, every one,
all waved me good-bye. They jumped into my cars
and drove away under the smoke-smuggered stars.

Now all that was left 'neath the bad-smelling sky
was my big empty factory . . .
the Lorax . . .
and I.

THNEEDS
THNEEDS

The Lorax said nothing. Just gave me a glance . . .
just gave me a very sad, sad backward glance . . .
as he lifted himself by the seat of his pants.
And I'll never forget the grim look on his face
when he heisted himself and took leave of this place,
through a hole in the smog, without leaving a trace.

And all that the Lorax left here in this mess
was a small pile of rocks, with the one word . . .
"UNLESS."
Whatever *that* meant, well I just couldn't guess.

That was long, long ago.
But each day since that day
I've sat here and worried
and worried away.
Through the years, while my buildings
have fallen apart,
I've worried about it
with all of my heart.

"But *now*," says the Once-ler,
"Now that *you're* here,
the word of the Lorax seems perfectly clear.
UNLESS someone like you
cares a whole awful lot,
nothing is going to get better.
It's not.

The ONCE-LER

"SO . . .
Catch!" calls the Once-ler.
He lets something fall.
"It's a Truffula Seed.
It's the last one of all!
You're in charge of the last of the Truffula Seeds.
And Truffula Trees are what everyone needs.
Plant a new Truffula. Treat it with care.
Give it clean water. And feed it fresh air.
Grow a forest. Protect it from axes that hack.
Then the Lorax
and all of his friends
may come back."

SCRAMBLED EGGS SUPER!

I don't like to brag and I don't like to boast,
Said Peter T. Hooper, but speaking of toast
And speaking of kitchens and ketchup and cake
And kettles and stoves and the stuff people bake . . .
Well, I don't like to brag, but I'm telling you, Liz,
That speaking of cooks, I'm the best that there is!
Why, only last Tuesday, when mother was out
I really cooked something worth talking about!

You see, I was sitting here, resting my legs
And I happened to pick up a couple of eggs
And I sort of got thinking – it's sort of a shame
That scrambled eggs always taste always the same.

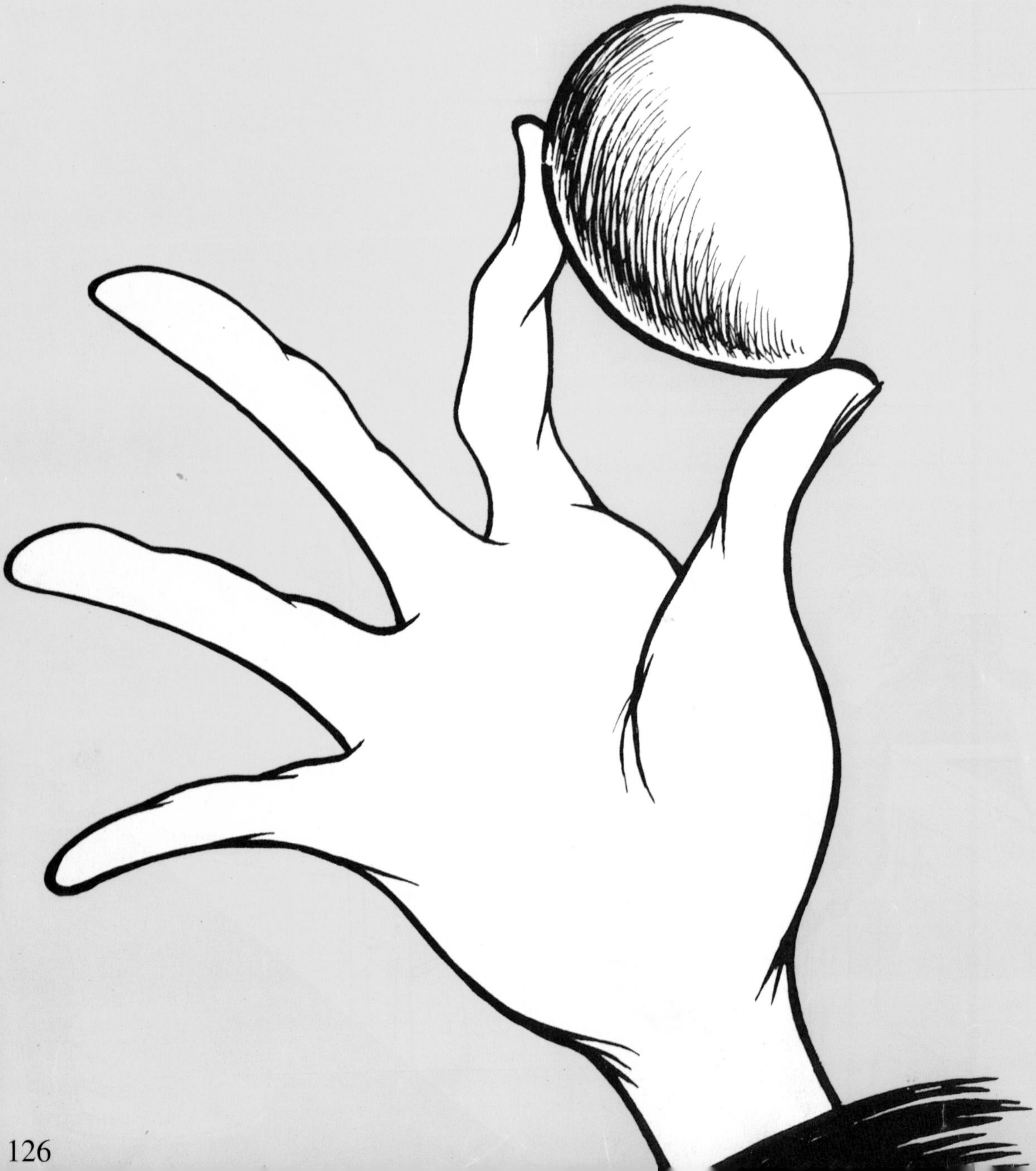

And that's because ever since goodness knows when,
They've always been made from the eggs of a *hen*.
Just a plain common hen! What a dumb thing to use
With all of the *other* fine eggs you could choose!

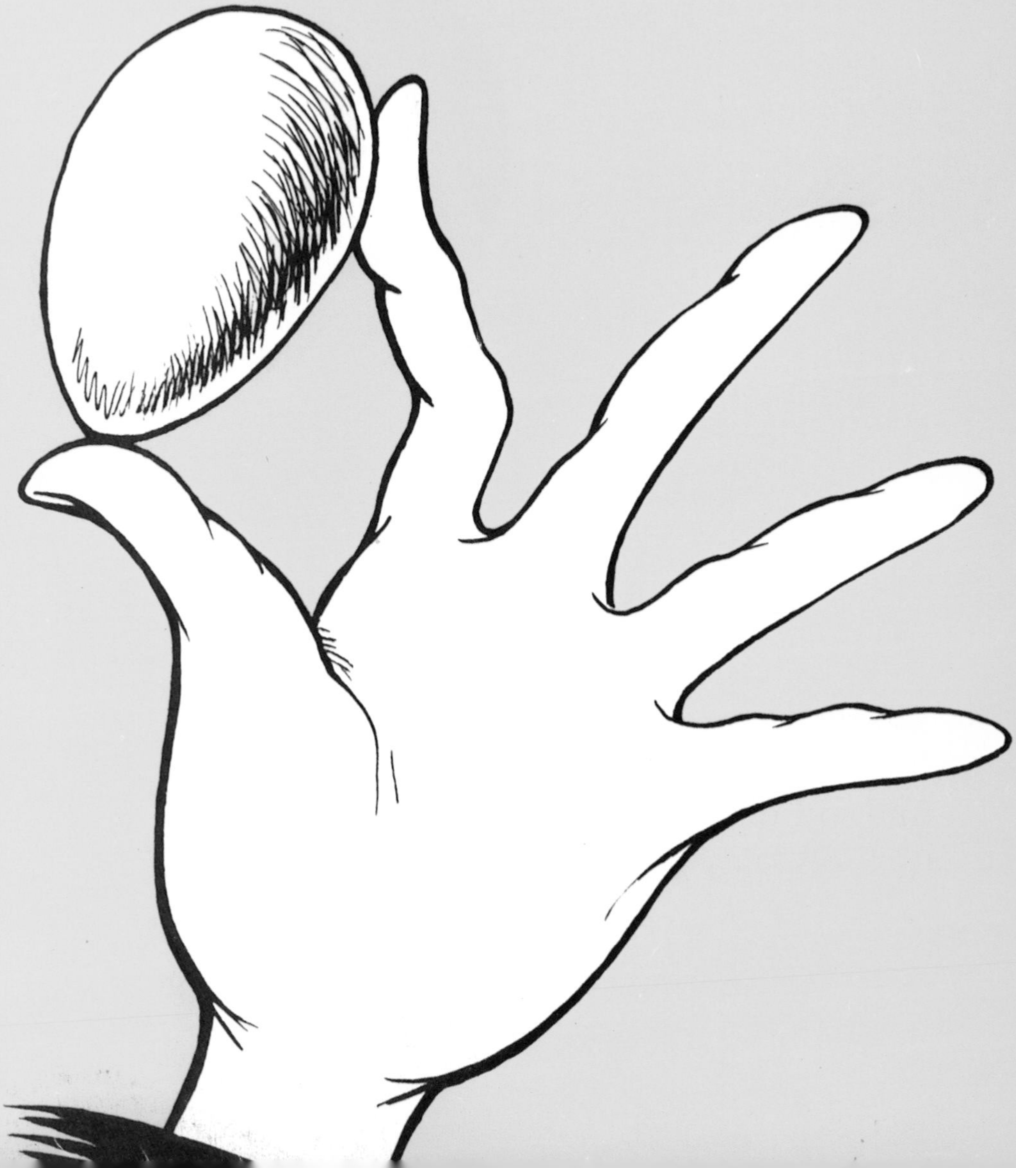

And so I decided that, just for a change,
I'd scramble a *new* kind of egg on the range.
Some fine fancy eggs that no other cook cooks
Like the eggs of the Ruffle-Necked Sala-ma-goox!

And while I was lugging them back to the house
I happened to notice a Tizzle-Topped Grouse
In a tree down the street. And I knew from her looks
That her egg and the egg of the Sala-ma-goox
Ought to mix mighty well; ought to taste simply super
When scrambled together by Peter T. Hooper.

So I took those eggs home and I frizzled 'em up.
And I added some sugar. Two thirds of a cup.
And a small pinch of pepper. And also a pound
Of horseradish sauce that was sitting around.
And also some nuts.
Then I tasted the stuff
And it tasted quite fine,
But not quite fine enough.

To make the best scramble that's ever been made
A cook has to hook the best eggs ever laid.
So I drove to the country, quite rather far out,
And studied the birds that were flitting about.
I looked with great care at a Mop-Noodled Finch.
I looked at a Beagle-Beaked-Bald-Headed Grinch.
And, also, I looked at a Shade-Roosting Quail
Who was roosting right under a Lass-a-lack's tail.
And I looked at a Spritz and a Flannel-Wing Jay.
But I just didn't stop. I kept right on my way
'Cause they didn't have eggs. They weren't laying that day.

Then, suddenly . . . *Boy!* Up that hill a short space . . .
Birds! They were laying all over the place!
Great happy gay families with uncles and cousins
All laying fine strictly fresh eggs by the dozens!

Why, I'd have a scramble *more* super than super!
Scrambled eggs Super-dee-Dooper-dee-Booper
Special de luxe à-la-Peter T. Hooper!

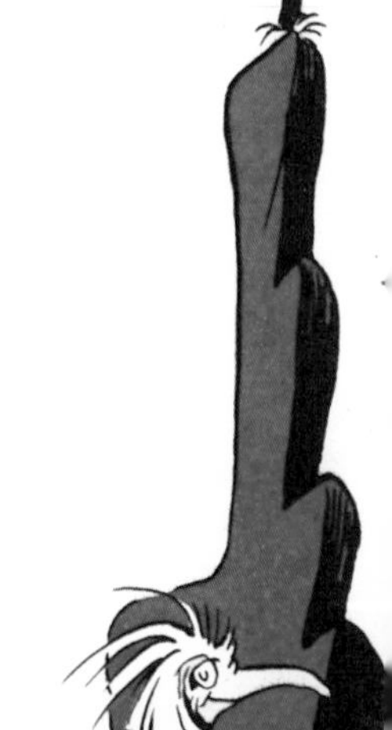

I picked out the eggs in a most careful way.
I only picked those that I knew were Grade-A.
I only took eggs from the very best fowls.
So I didn't take eggs from the Twiddler Owls
'Cause I knew that the eggs of those fellows who twiddle
Taste sort of like dust from inside a bass fiddle.

I went for the kind that were mellow and sweet
And the world's sweetest eggs are the eggs of the Kweet
Which is due to those very sweet trout which they eat
And those trout . . . well, *they're* sweet 'cause they only eat Blogs
And Blogs, after all, are the world's sweetest frogs
And the reason *they're* sweet is, whenever they lunch
It's always the world's sweetest bees that they munch
And the reason no bees can be sweeter than these . . .
They only eat blossoms off Beezlenut Trees
And these Beezlenut Blossoms are sweeter than sweet
And that's why I nabbed several eggs from the Kweet.

But I passed up the eggs of a bird called a Stroodel
Who's sort of a stork, but with fur like a poodle.
For they say that the eggs of this kind of a stork
Are gooey like glue and they stick to your fork,
And the yolks of these eggs, I am told, taste like fleece
While the whites taste like very old bicycle grease.

The places I hiked to! The roads that I rambled
To find the best eggs that have ever been scrambled!
I hunted new birds along wild tangled trails,
Through gullies and gulches, down dingles and dales.
I wriggled my way and I crawled at a creep
Through a forest of ferns that was forty miles deep.
And I mushed through the brush till I found a fine Kwigger
Whose eggs are as big as a pin head, no bigger.

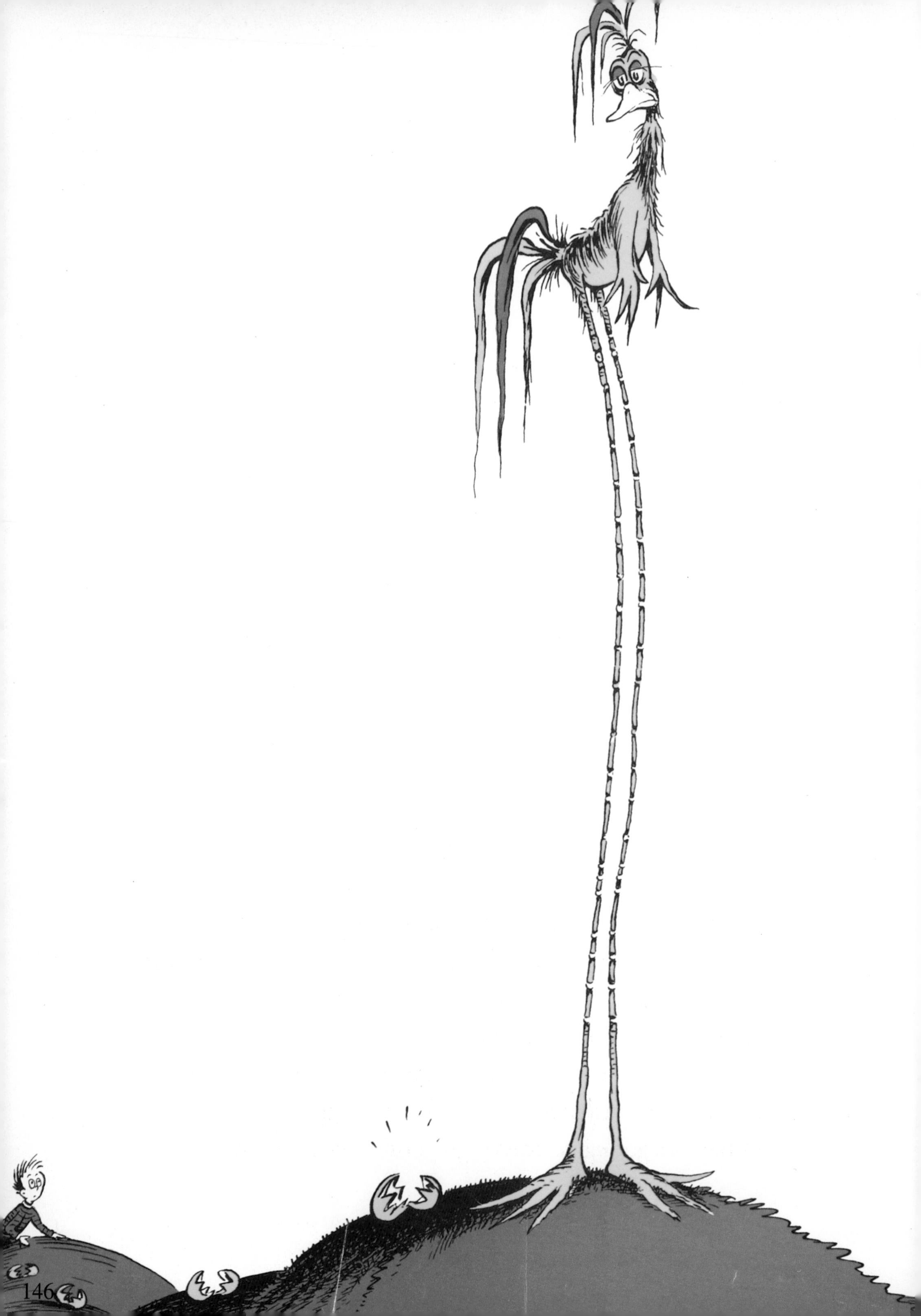

Then I went for the eggs of a Long-Legger Kwong.
Now this Kwong . . . well, she's built just a little bit wrong,
For her legs are so terribly, terribly long
That she has to lay eggs twenty feet in the air
And they drop, with a plop, to the ground from up there!
So unless you can catch 'em before the eggs crash
You haven't got eggs. You've got Long-Legger hash.

Eggs! I'd collected three hundred and two!
But I needed still more! And I suddenly knew
That the job was too big for one fellow to do.
So I telegraphed north to some friends near Fa-Zoal
Which is ten miles or so just beyond the North Pole.
And they all of them jumped in their Katta-ma-Side,
Which is sort of a boat made of sea-leopard's hide,
Which they sailed out to sea to go looking for Grice,
Which is sort of a bird which lays eggs on the ice,
Which they grabbed with a tool which is known as a Squitsch,
'Cause those eggs are too cold to be touched without which.

And while they were sending those eggs, I got word of
A bird that does something that's almost unheard of !
It's hard to believe, but this bird called the Pelf
Lays eggs that are three times as big as herself!
How that Pelf ever learned such a difficult trick
I never found out. But I found that egg quick.
And I managed to get it down out of the nest
And home to the kitchen along with the rest.

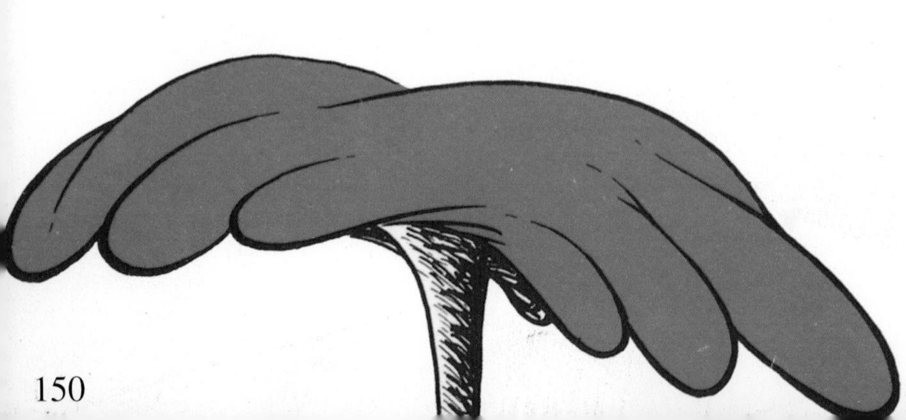

But I didn't stop then, 'cause I knew of some ducks
By the name of the Single-File Zummzian Zuks
Who stroll, single file, through the mountains of Zumms
Quite oddly enough, with their eggs on their thumbs,
And some fellows in Zummz whom I happened to know
Just happened to capture a thousand or so,
And they wrapped up their eggs and they mailed them by air
Marked Special Delivery, Handle with Care.

I needed *more* helpers! And so for assistance
I called up a fellow, named Ali, long distance,
And Ali, as soon as he hung up the phone,
Picked up a small basket and started alone
To climb the steep crags and jags of Mt. Strookoo
To fetch me the egg of a Mt. Strookoo Cuckoo.
Now these Mt. Strookoo Cuckoos
Are rather small gals . . .

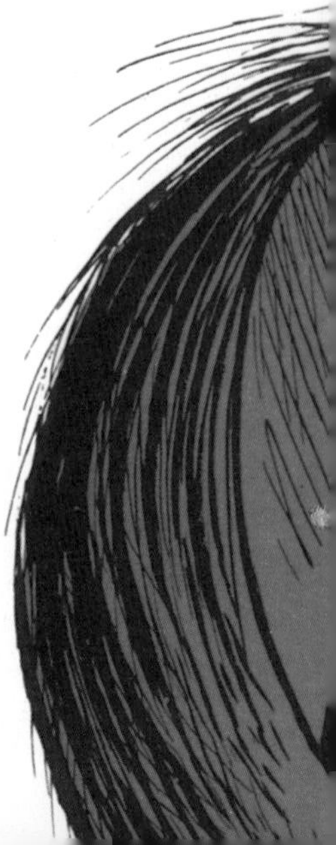

But these Mt. Strookoo Cuckoos have lots of big pals!
They dived from the skies with wild cackling shrieks
And they jabbed at his legs and they stabbed at his cheeks
With their yammering, klammering, hammering beaks,
But Ali, brave Ali, he fought his way through
And he sent me that egg as I knew he would do
For my Scrambled Eggs Super-dee-Dooper-dee-Booper
Special de luxe à-la-Peter T. Hooper!

In the meanwhile, of course, I was keeping real busy
Collecting the eggs of the three-eyelashed Tizzy.
They're quite hard to reach, so I rode on the top
Of a Ham-ikka-Schnim-ikka-Schnam-ikka Schnopp.

Then I found a great flock of South-West-Facing Cranes
And I guess they've got something that's wrong with their brains.
For this kind of a crane, when she's guarding her nest,
Will always stand facing precisely South West.
So to get at those eggs wasn't hard in the least.
I came from behind. From, precisely, North East.

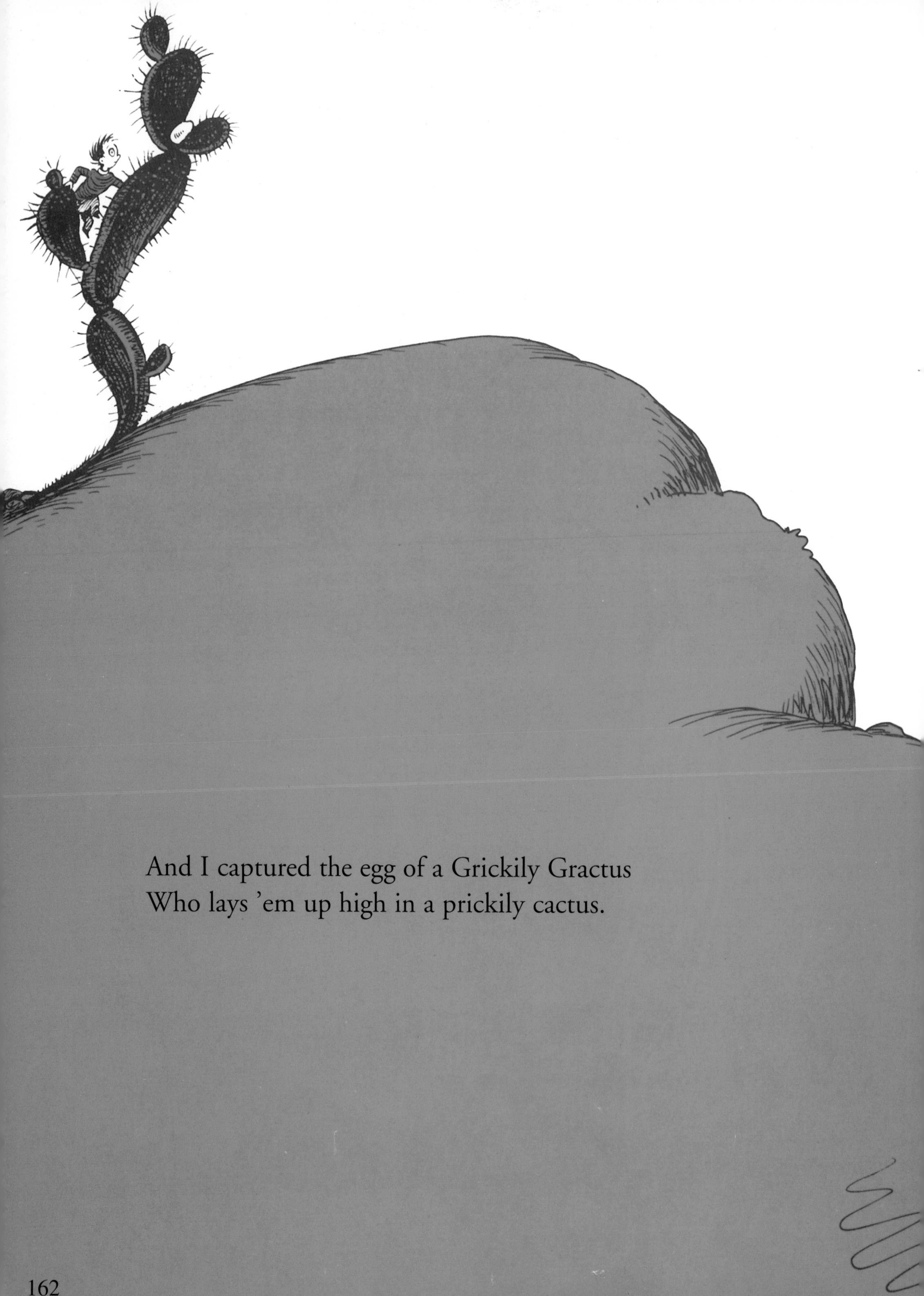

And I captured the egg of a Grickily Gractus
Who lays 'em up high in a prickily cactus.

Then I went for some Ziffs. They're exactly like Zuffs,
But the Ziffs live on cliffs and the Zuffs live on bluffs.
And, seeing how bluffs are exactly like cliffs,
It's mighty hard telling the Zuffs for the Ziffs.
But I *know* that the egg that I got from the bluffs,
If it wasn't a Ziff's from the cliffs, was a Zuff's.

Now I needed the egg of a Moth-Watching Sneth
Who's a bird who's so big she scares people to death!
And this awful big bird . . . Well, the reason they name her
The Moth-Watching Sneth is 'cause that's how they tame her.
She likes watching moths. Sort of quiets her mind.
And while she is watching you sneak up behind
And you yank out her egg. So I got one, of course,
With the help of some friends and a very fast horse.

If you want to get eggs you can't buy at a store,
You have to do things never thought of before.
Why, to get at the egg of one very small Dawf,
We had to pry all of one mountain top off!

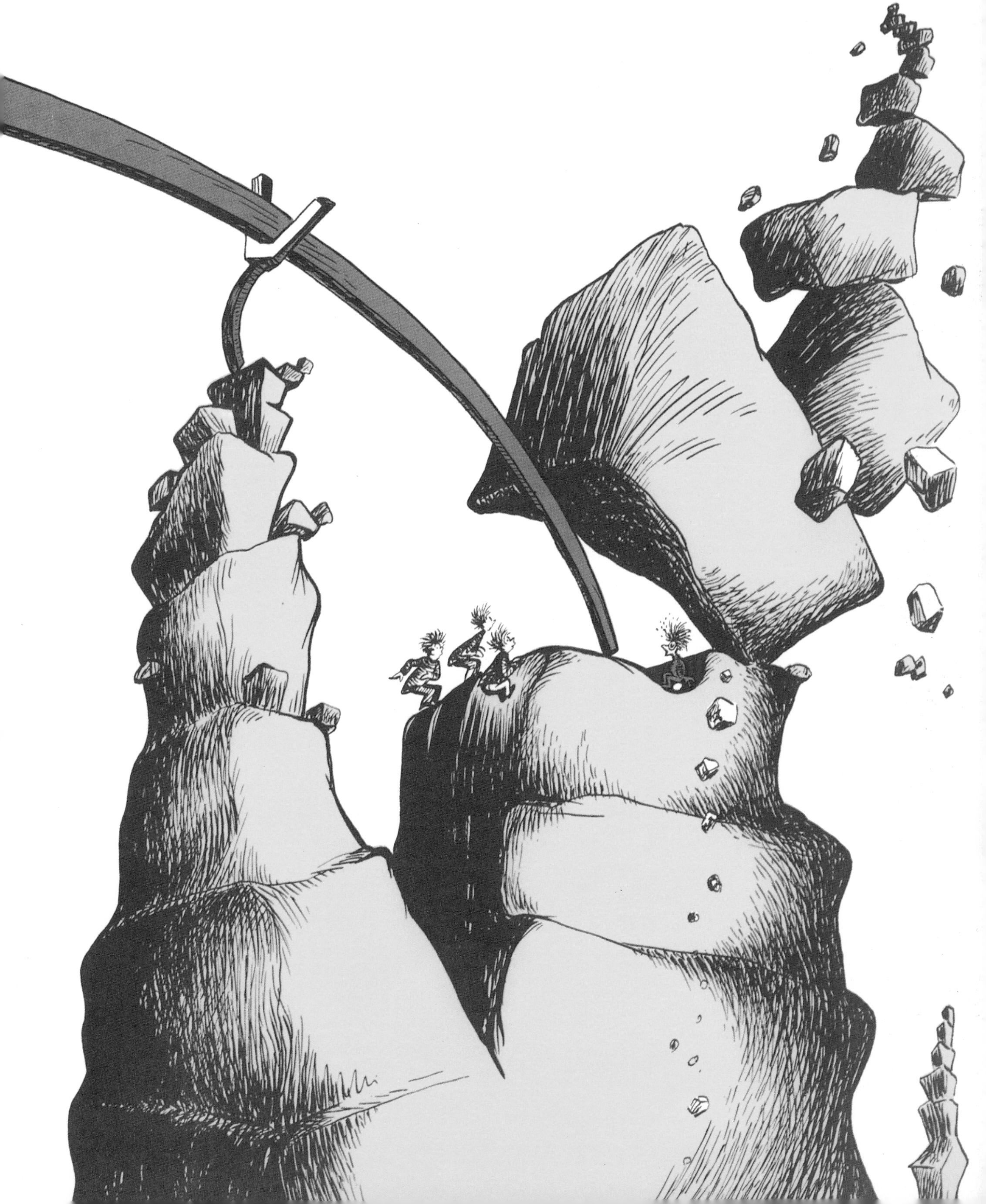

Then I heard of some birds who lay eggs, if you please,
That taste like the air in the holes in Swiss cheese
And they live in big Zinzibar-Zanzibar trees.
So I ordered a tree full. The job was immense,
But I needed those eggs, and said hang the expense!

I still needed one more! And I saved it for last . . .
The egg of the frightful Bombastic Aghast!
And that bird is so mean and that bird is so fast
That I had to escape on a Jill-ikka-Jast
A fleet-footed beast who can run like a deer
But looks sort of different. You steer him by ear.

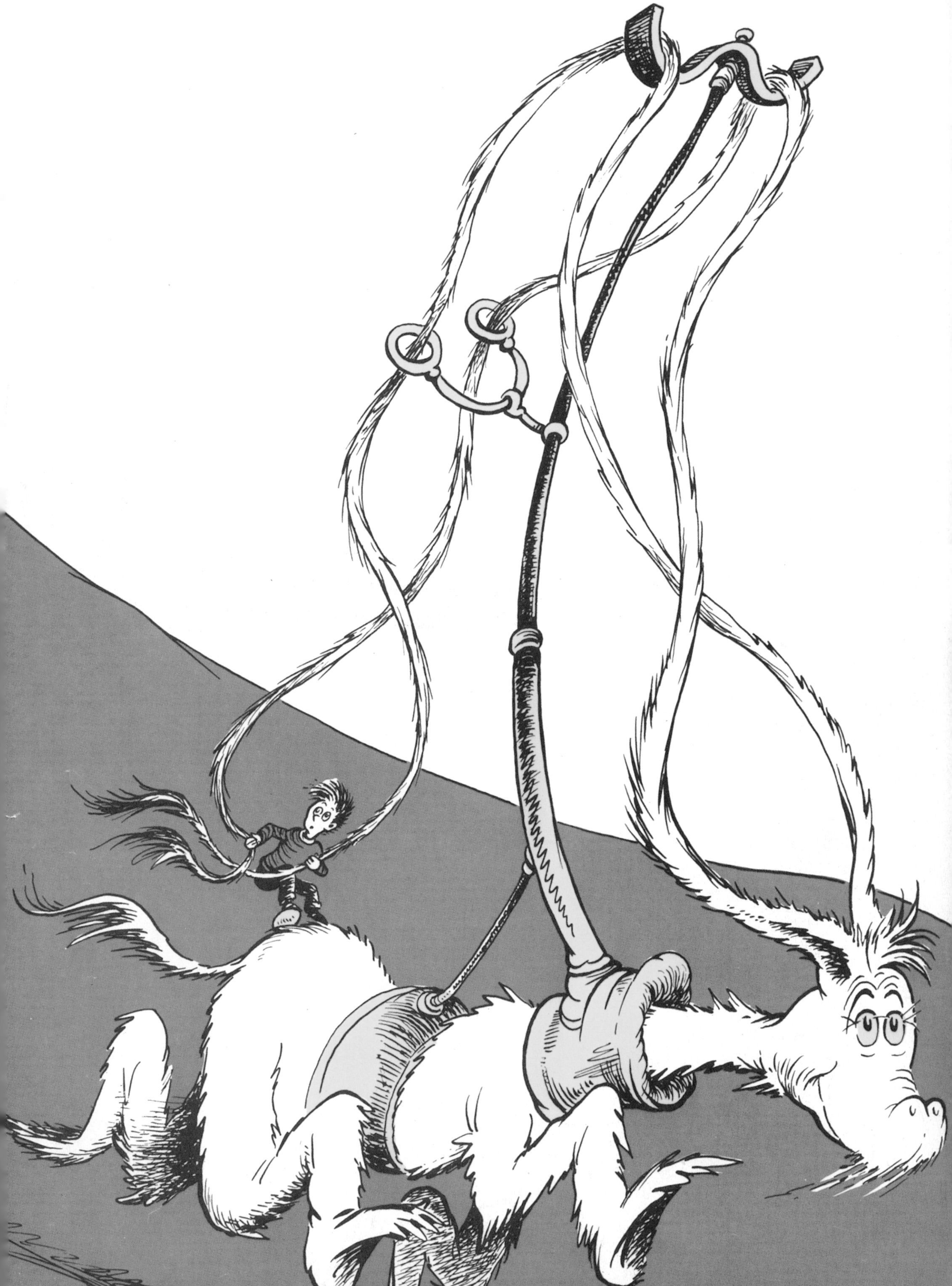